To: Fran

Forrest

Happenstance

Forrest A. Abell

Happenstance

Forrest A. Abell

Noble House
Baltimore, Maryland

Happenstance

Library of Congress
Cataloging in Publication Data
ISBN 1-56167-343-9

Library of Congress Card Catalog Number:
96-071908

Published by

8019 Belair Road, Suite 10
Baltimore, Maryland 21236

Manufactured in the United States of America

Prologue

This purely fictitious book is a poverty to riches story.

Happenstance as defined by the dictionary:
"A chance occurrence, not planned, not expected."

This book called *Happenstance* is the figment of a young fellow's runaway imagination, while searching for an escape from poverty. It is about strange and timely happenings of fantasy, factors of life and unusual sexual encounters, fictitiously speaking, leading to financial success. The more you read of this story, the closer you will get to understanding the usual, rather than the unusual.

Happenstance is a **fictional story**! Any reference to any person living or dead is purely coincidental and all places and things are fictional. It is fiction, fantasy, facts of life, strange and the untimely sexual encounters leading to financial success.

It is the story of a boy born in mountain country during the early part of the twentieth century. The mountains were in the clouds in the morning, and when the fog cleared, it revealed the beauty of the evergreen trees, and the blossoming hawthorn trees on the south side of the mountain made it a fairy wonderland.

The fast flowing brook and the fields of waving vegetation were our scene as we looked from the living room window of our six room house. It was best termed a renovated miner's shanty. At least it kept us from being homeless. It had no insulation to protect us from the cold winters when the temperature would sometimes go as low as forty degrees below zero. We had a cast iron cooking stove and a pot bellied heating stove. During the winter, someone had to stay up all night to keep coal in the firebox or the house would get cold beyond a tolerable level.

The biggest problem was that there were six children and a father and mother to share the small amount of food that was available. This was an era of poverty. The coal mines had been worked out and about the only employment was seasonal farm work and occasional lumbering. In those days there was no refrigeration for storage of food. In fact, there was no electricity in the village until about 1934. We had to can and dry food for the winter. We had a root cellar where we could keep those kinds of items. One of the interesting things was that we could bury cabbage in the earth by mounding the earth over the heads of the cabbage, but we had to leave the tips of the roots from the upside down cabbage exposed to the air. The frost line depth was three feet, but the one foot of earth covering the cabbage kept it from freezing. It created its own heat. Another interesting revelation, yellow onions would not freeze in an open attic unless you touched one of the onions. We stored them in separate piles and when you took one from the pile you had to take all from that group. That mystery goes with the one that causes your eyeglasses not to steam up if you walk between areas with a large temperature difference backwards, it works. I don't know why, and I do not have the answer.

One of the earliest happenings that shook me up took place one evening when I was lying on the floor in front of the pot belly heating stove. The coal was burning and giving off comforting heat, when all of a sudden there was an explosion in the firebox of the stove, at the same time I was wondering what life was all about. I was about four years old. My brother had died a few weeks before and I was listening to the dogs howling. Someone had said that when the dogs were restless, something bad was going to happen. So I really wondered about the untimely explosion. The reason for the explosion was that one of my older brothers had thrown a rifle cartridge, which had not fired, into the coal bin and it finally got shoveled into the stove. When the cartridge reached a high temperature, it exploded . . . but why at the precise moment when I was wondering what life was all about?

The next thing that happened: There was a mirror of about twelve by eighteen inches in a picture frame hanging over the wash basin in the kitchen. The cord that held it up was sort of in a condition to break and while I was thinking about how much longer it could last, the cord broke and the mirror fell into the wash basin, but it did not break. I was beginning to think I was jinxing things.

I suppose I was considered a small boy with large tales

because one day during a lightning storm, I went into the kitchen to get a drink of water, and lightning struck our neighbor's barn. The barn was engulfed in a blue haze and then broke out into flames. I ran into the living room and told my parents. They said, "Sure, sure," just like it had not happened. I begged them to come and see if they could help put out the fire. They finally believed me and responded to assist the neighbor in trying to extinguish the flames, but the barn burned to the ground.

One of the strange things about this incident was that the neighbor put the harness and bridle onto the horse before he led it out of the burning building. I asked why he took time to do that. He replied, "A horse will not leave a burning building without a harness." Maybe it's true. I suggest you ask your veterinarian.

Life was very hard for children, for there was little to do and always not enough food. To add to our woes, my father tore down the large building that had been a drying shed, where we could ride our little wagon and roller skate in the winter. He said it was a fire hazard, but I learned later this was done to reduce the property tax and insurance.

I was now about eight years old and every child had to go to school from the age of eight to the age of sixteen. It was an enforceable law. We had to walk a mile through the fields and woods on a foot-beaten path covered with snow and mud. There was no improved road. We had very little clothing and most of the time we had no boots. The snow was sometimes two feet deep. There was no excuse for missing school. We had to go regardless of the weather. (School buses were unheard of in those days.) Many times we had to go to school without breakfast and we hardly ever had anything for lunch. At supper time we ate whatever we could find. It was not our parents' fault, they did the best they could with what they had, but now I ask myself, why did they keep having children? I suppose it was like the old saying, the rich get richer and the poor get children.

I was glad to be able to go to school, and I was eager to learn. Also, at school I was a part of something, one of the kids. By the time I arrived at the school house, someone had been there and had a big fire burning in the pot belly stove. I was able to get my clothing dried off by standing so close to the stove that steam rose from the garments.

It was a two room schoolhouse, with grades one through four in one room and five through eight in the other. The teachers were very good, which made learning easy. There was strict discipline in those days. If you got a spanking in school, you got another one when your parents found out, so the need for correction was minimal. We always had a Valentines Day and a Christmas play. Everyone had to participate, and each student learned a saying or performed something for the play. The parents were invited to the recitation, so we did our best for them. The older students would go into the woods and fetch a large Christmas tree. Each one of us was required to hand make an ornament and put it on the tree. We exchanged gifts, using whatever we could find, as long as it was wrapped and put under the tree. There was a cute little girl with long curly hair that always opened the Christmas play by coming out onto the stage and saying, "What are you looking at me for, I haven't anything to say, so just content your happy hearts and listen to the play," then she would dash off the stage and the play would begin. She was so bouncy and cute that she got everyone's attention.

When we graduated to the fifth grade they had what was called a Box Social. The girls would prepare a box of food for two people, wrap it with decorative paper and bring it to school. The boxes were put on the table without names on them. They were auctioned off to the boys. The girl's name was inside the box and the boy that was the successful bidder had the pleasure of dining with the girl that had prepared the goodies. All went well until some of the wealthy boys found out which pretty girl had prepared which box and they bid much higher than the poor boys could bid. One of the boys even saved all year in order to out bid for the most beautiful girl's goodies. The auctioneer stopped the bidding at thirty dollars. (In those days that was an average month's wages.) The school principal declared the Box Social abolished. It was leading to real trouble, especially implying that some students were better than others.

There was one big boy in the eighth grade that liked to hit the students in the lower grades. He especially liked to hit me because I was frail, undernourished and sort of weak. I told my father about him and asked him for his help. What could I do? My father said, "What do you want me to do, beat up on the kid for you?" I said, "No, but what could I do?" He said, "The next time he hits you, hit him right on the jaw as hard as you can. Don't swing, just put your weight behind a hard right, and flatten him." I said, "Then I will be in big trouble." I couldn't believe what happened. I did just as I was told and hit him as hard as I could. He fell to the ground and was embarrassed to be humiliated by anyone. He did not challenge me again and was very careful who he picked on in the future.

My first employment: A nearby farmer asked me and my older brother if we would hoe thistles out of his cornfield for a dollar a day and two meals. We quickly agreed because two hungry boys could really do justice to farm food. We worked diligently and ate like horses. At the end of the first day, we asked the farmer if we could have a dollar. He told us he paid once a week, on Saturday. We explained to the farmer, we wanted the money to buy a drum of Picnic Twist chewing tobacco (most of the young boys chewed tobacco in those days). The farmer paid us the dollar and we went to the tobacco store (with a forged signature, giving the store keeper permission to sell tobacco to a minor). The storekeeper said he would let us buy the tobacco but laughed at the note. He knew better, but he was safe from the law if he had a note. We were glad we had jobs because the Fourth of July was coming up and we would have money to buy lots of good things to eat and get some firecrackers like the rich kids always had.

The day before the Fourth we took our little red wagon and went to the grocery store, which was about a mile away. We ordered a large watermelon and a case of Coca-Cola, which came in glass bottles and sat in a wooden case. We ordered milk chocolate, cookies and firecrackers plus a few other goodies. The grocer said, "This is a lot of food and drink. Do you have any idea of how you are going to pay for it?" We said, "No problem," and presented our bank roll. He was surprised and apologized for his comment, but he asked just where did two boys get that much cash. We told him we earned it working on a farm. He said, "Okay, here is the order, but I will have to verify where you got the money." Most of the people in town did not have that much extra cash. The grocer did check up on us and after that he would even give us credit until payday if we wanted it.

We had no running water at our home, so we took the melon and the soda up to the water spring, which was nine hundred feet away, and cooled it. We had a big joke at our house, we had running water, the only thing was that you had to run to fetch it. It was a memorable Fourth of July because our parents and other brothers and sisters were able to share in the good time.

After the autumn crops were harvested we would go into the old mine on Saturday to get coal for the stoves that would keep us warm during the long cold winter. We only mined coal on Saturday because we were required to attend school during the week days. Our parents were very religious and we were not allowed to do unnecessary work on Sunday. The coal mine was on the farmer's property and had been leased to a big coal dealer that shipped coal by the train load. The mine had been what is known as being worked out, that is, all the coal that could be safely removed had been.

The coal that the miners left behind was called pillars. It was good coal but had to be mined by an experienced miner. We would take as much coal as we could get before the roof of the mine would start to cave in, then we would make a fast escape, back to where it was safe. It was sort of like playing pistol roulette. However, we were hardly ever at risk because we got a warning and had to obey it, pronto. One time, while we were retreating, I took the horse and coal car and the farmer followed me to safety. When we got outside my brother was nowhere to be seen; we concluded that he had been crushed to death. While we were grieving, he came walking along the hillside. We were relieved and asked him how he escaped. He said there was no time to help us or do anything and he just wanted to get out of our way so we could escape. He ran out the airshaft corridor. It was the best thing for him to do, but it certainly gave us a scare that took a long time to get over.

My brother and I were always trying to improve something. There was a fast flowing trout stream about a hundred feet from our house. We enjoyed fishing and catching turtles. The thought occurred to us to remove a lot of rocks and earth from the bottom of the stream and make a swimming hole. There was one part of the stream that was obscured by a high bank of terrain. That is where we decided to make the deep spot because we could skinny-dip and no one could see us. Also, we could build a big bonfire against the hillside and get warm after swimming. The water was warm, but in that part of the country as soon as the sun went down the temperature would drop drastically in a short time.

It took us all summer to complete the hole. It was nine feet deep when we finished. We installed a diving board and really had a lot of fun.

One of the neighbor boys would wade around the edge of the river, but refused to learn to swim. One day, he was sitting on the end of the diving board and two of us decided to run out and drag him along into the water. Right there and then, he swam. I thought he would be angry because he had a short temper, but instead he thanked us for getting him over his fear of the water.

One evening a few of the neighborhood girls came down and took our clothing, for a joke, and ran away with it. They only went to the top of the hill and after a while tossed the clothes back to us. In the meantime we had to stay in deep water. I suppose this was the beginning of puppy love.

One of the events we really enjoyed was in the autumn, when we would have corn roasts. We would build a big wood fire and get fresh ears of corn right off the cornstalk, that way it was moist and easy to roast. We would peel off all but one husk and stand the corn up against a stone where the heat from the fire would roast it to a golden brown. Then we would put lots of salt and butter onto it and enjoy the treat. It was also a very good way for the poor neighbor kids to get a good meal. Sometimes we would roast potatoes and chestnuts, which were plentiful.

All we had to do was harvest them.

One of the exciting happenings was a real thriller (after it was over). The farmer had a three-year-old mare that had an injury which had to heal before she could be, what horse people called, broken. A term meaning they subject the animal to a work harness and a bridle. She had gotten very fat because she ate a lot and, of course, didn't work.

One day she was standing by a farm wagon. I decided to get onto her back to see what she would do. I found out in a hurry. She took off like a scared rabbit and headed out of the farm toward town. Right in front of my parents' home she decided to unload me. She did a very wild bucking bronco act. All I had to hold on to was a small mane of hair.

Thank God we never had a saddle on the farm, we always rode bareback. I knew if she threw me off she would paw me because she was just plain scared. Fortunately, none of my family saw what was happening.

She decided to run back to the barn stall. I knew when she turned to get into the barn I would be scraped off. As she made the turn, I let go and landed into a well aged manure pile, right into it up to my elbows. She went into the barn and I went to the now much appreciated swimming hole and washed off, which I really needed.

One of the neighbor boys and I used to race the horses. His father was a horse trader and from time-to-time he would get some pretty good ones. The farmer that I worked for had a small fast stepping horse that we used to pull the buggy. It could run like the wind. The neighbor boy challenged me to a race. I told him there was no average horse that could compete with him. He insisted, and the race was on. The horse I was riding ran away with me. I could not hold him. I had a straight bit bridle and no matter how hard I pulled, he just ran faster. I tried in vain to control him. It is a wonder that he did not break his web, that is what usually happens when a horse exerts himself too much. He ran until he came to a rail fence in front of him and he stopped short. I immediately dismounted and held on to the bridle. He calmed down very easily. I suspect he had been a race horse at some previous time and when we began the race, he did what he was supposed to do— WIN. I was grateful that he was alive and that I was not thrown. That ended my ever agreeing to racing again.

When I was fourteen years old and in the seventh grade, we children went to a Methodist Church Sunday School. Everyone was eager to have a perfect attendance because if we did not miss a Sunday for a year, we got gold bars for our attendance badges. One day the Sunday School teacher asked for volunteers to go into the woods and get a large Christmas tree for the church.

Of course, my brother and I decided we could do it. The woods were about a mile away and most of the return was down a slight grade, only a short distance from the church was up a steep grade. We took some rope to make harnesses and a boy scout hatchet and went into the woods. We selected a tree about fourteen feet tall and cut it down, attached our ropes to the tree and started for the church. The snow was not too deep in the woods because a lot of it had fallen onto the tree branches and stayed on them.

When we arrived at the open field, the snow was almost a foot deep and it had started to rain and sleet. All this precipitation built up on the tree and the footing got slippery and we came close to getting bogged down. We would not give up and kept inching along. We were getting wet and also very tired, but we decided we must not fail.

We finally arrived at the foot of the upgrade. At this time we decided to take a short cut through the cemetery, which we did. We tried not to cross any graves and finally arrived at the church, fortunately there were some men there to get the tree into the vestibule where the ice and snow could melt off it.

I was very ambitious. The road into the farm from the country road was about a half a mile of just plain earth. When it rained the ruts got so deep that we had to use a horse to pull the automobile through the mud until we got onto the main road. After we plowed and harrowed the farm fields, there were a lot of small stones to be picked up. I would make a wagon bed out of planks and load the stones on to it. Then I would dump the stones onto the mud road. After dinner, I would break the big ones and place all of them into a six foot wide group, about six inches high. Then I would shovel earth over the stones as a binder and at the same time make a water drain ditch along the sides of the road. I was surprised that the neighbors, who would benefit from the road, never once asked me if they could help. I actually built a quarter mile of a good road before the county completed it. It took me about a year to build the part that I did.

I got the idea to build a stone shack in the woods. I decided to make it ten feet by ten feet and seven feet high. All went well until I got up to around four feet and then the walls became quite shaky. I decided to discontinue the project, lest someone get killed if it collapsed, which I'm sure would have happened.

I tried to build an automobile garage, partly under the earth, on a small lot which I had purchased for fifteen dollars from an elderly neighbor that had no further use for it. I finally abandoned the project due to lack of funds to complete the job.

I suppose that nature has decreed that sooner or later, we are destined to have a sexual experience, but mine was to be a very unusual happenstance. I certainly did not expect it to happen with the person it did or at the time it did.

There was a neighbor lady that had never married because she had a mother that needed a lot of care. After her mother passed away she lived in the house alone. She had a rose and vegetable garden as well as a lot of shrubbery around the house, and she always appeared to be happy just living by herself and minding her own business. She was a good neighbor and was always ready to help anyone in need. I never heard her say a bad word about anyone. I believe she was about fifty years of age, which to a boy of sixteen seemed ancient. She looked old by my way of thinking and the thought of getting that friendly with her never entered my mind.

One day I was on my way home from high school and she was in the doorway. She asked me if I could take a look at her screen door. The dog had jumped up onto it and pulled the screen from under the trim. I told her that I would come out after dinner and repair it because I had to get to the farm to get the barn chores done right away.

I took some carpenter tools and proceeded to reinstall the screen. All I had to do was loosen the trim, put the screen back in place and tack the trim back on. It only took a few minutes to do the repair and she said it looked as good as new. She said that she didn't have any money to pay me, but she had made a big lemon meringue pie for me. I thanked her and said that I did not expect to be paid for doing such a nice neighbor a good turn. I ate a piece of the pie (which was better than I had ever tasted). She was standing in the middle of the kitchen floor and I got up from the table and told her how good the pie was, complimented her on being a good cook as well as a good neighbor and friend.

She said that she saw me going out the road the other day holding hands with a little girl. I told her that was only puppy love, nothing serious. I said, "You know her, she is my neighbor's oldest daughter, but she is only twelve years old." I explained that I carried her books home from school and we went around together, but I had no other interest in her, she was too young for me. I told her that I had never even kissed her, in fact, I had never kissed a girl. I didn't know what it was like. I asked her a dumb question, had she ever been kissed? Imagine being fifty years old and never being kissed. Anyway, she said she had often been kissed, but not that way. I understood what she meant. It wasn't smart to be asking questions like that, but we were friends and neighbors and I felt at ease asking my dumb questions.

I still can't believe that I was stupid enough to ask her if she would mind if I kissed her, just to see what it would be like. She said she didn't mind and I put my arms around her, in fact she was so big that my arms only went half way around her. I gave her a big kiss and said, "That is not so bad, let's do it again." She agreed, and we had a long drawn out kiss with meaning.

At this point I was getting confused and began wondering what I was becoming involved in, it was so far out of place and reality. My face got redder and I kissed her again and again. She was kissing like she wanted more and the feeling was mutual. She had a beautiful yellow dress on and it was quite thin and loose fitting. I could feel her body, especially her large breasts, touching me! Whatever influenced me to push the dress over one shoulder at a time is beyond my wildest imagination, but I did it. Her dress fell to the floor and WOW, she did not have anything on under it. She was naked!

At this time I was in a quandary as to know what to do. I knew what I wanted to do, but I was confused and bewildered. I said, "Let's set on the sofa for a few minutes."

She said she did not have a sofa, but we could sit on the edge of the bed, which was just across the hall. I said that would be fine. We sat on the edge of the bed and did some more kissing. I became more anxious for something to happen. I pushed her back on to the bed and said, "I better take my shoes off so I do not get your bed soiled." I slipped out of my farmer's overalls and got into bed with her.

She didn't resist me and we kept on kissing and touching. Finally, I tried to do something that I had never done before, but double WOW! I was ready and anxious. She said, "NO, NO, NO, You don't do that." I tried harder, but she resisted. She said she could get into trouble legally and otherwise. I tried every possible trick word and a few lies. I suggested that I get a prophylactic and then we could be active and safe. She said, "Absolutely NO." She said her friend had gotten pregnant that way, so just forget it.

I asked her what she had in mind when we first got involved. She said that she had gotten carried away by the same driving force that I had. It was all new to her, she had never gone this far before. She said that we could enjoy tumbling and kissing, but that was as far as I could go. I told her that I thoroughly enjoyed tumbling and kissing, and being able to go to bed and cuddle in the nude was wonderful. But how much of it could I take without some satisfaction and relief? She said that it was up to me, but that was absolutely as far as she would go, take it or leave it! I backed off my begging and told her I would like to continue the good times in bed. It was all I had, and life was not offering me anything but poverty and despair, so as out of context as it was, I wanted to continue the relationship with or without sex.

After about a half hour of cuddling and consoling each other, I said I would have to go home because I had to get up early to do barn chores before I went to school. She said, "I will never see you again." I said, "Why not?" She said it was because she took advantage of me and let herself get out of control. I said, "I was just as much to blame and maybe more so because I got over excited and would not control my desires." I said, "Let's blame it on nature and take it from there." She agreed, but said, "I know you won't come here anymore." I said, "I sure will. How about tomorrow night?" She said it was agreeable and we would have time to think about our wrong doings. I said I did not consider them wrong under the timely circumstances and that we were just two normal human beings reacting to what was natural. I had no regrets, none whatsoever. She said she felt terrible because she was afraid of getting us both into trouble, and she felt badly about getting me so worked up and then being selfish. I told her that I had let myself get out of control when I had no right. I said, "Let's just put it out of our minds and see what happens tomorrow night." She agreed, we kissed and said good night to each other. I went to the swimming hole for a good cooling off, then went home.

I was still excited when I got into bed and had a hard time getting to sleep. What in the world was I getting into, and where was it going, and where would it end? I was so confused.

The next morning when I went by her house, she was sitting by the window. She smiled and threw me a kiss. I smiled and threw her a kiss. That made my day of pondering a little easier to bear. I couldn't get her off my mind, not because of what I hoped to get, but because I was doing a really strange thing. I was glad that she did not say YES. It gave me time to decide if I really wanted to do it. I kept asking myself, "Do I or do I not?" And the answer always came up, "Yes I do." I felt I must find out what it was like, what it was all about.

17

All day, I kept thinking, tonight she will let me, how will I handle it, will it be as exciting as if we had done it the night before? When I thought about it, I became aroused. Then I would decide, if she says yes, maybe I should wait. The answer was always go for it, it is all you have. Don't let it pass you by. It will prepare you for a more normal encounter when it comes, and it will come because sex is a part of life.

Evening came and I went to her house and nervously tapped on the door. She was waiting for me, she invited me in and gave me a big hug and a kiss. It was a strange feeling, not like the first kiss, it was exciting, but I had a strange feeling. I kept asking myself, "What are you doing? Why?"

I said, "What do you want to do?" She said, "It is comfortable in bed, let's pop-in and hold each other and talk." I agreed, and in a few moments we were back in bed completely nude. I kissed her and caressed her, but somehow I could not get the courage to ask her to be real nice to me. We just held each other closely and sort of went into a trance. It was a very good feeling. Her body was against my body and quiet reigned.

After a while, I asked her if she had changed her mind about letting me have my way. She said she had not changed her mind but would think about doing it sometime in the future, not for a long time, however. She said I was too young and if she became pregnant it would be a real mess in a small town. Actually, I was pleased at her decision because it gave me more time to decide if I really wanted to get involved.

We would get together several nights a week and have the usual petting session, tumble, rock and roll, but the word sex did not come up. We both seemed to get a lot of good satisfaction from our new found excitement. It was hard for both of us because we wanted each other, but not in the worst way. She was able to keep me from getting too anxious because she could feel my body craving hers and she had the same feeling.

It was a glorious experience just doing what we were doing. After a few weeks, I suggested that we discontinue seeing each other every night, cool it. I said it was just too much for me to handle. She agreed, and begged me not to stop altogether. This seemed to work out better because the temptation was reduced to a tolerable level. However, the strong desire kept gnawing away at both of us. We would get so close, then back off. I was certain it would get the better of us in a moment of weakness, but that did not happen.

It was extremely exciting on the Fourth of July. We were in bed and the fireworks were beautiful from her window. Every time a boom would go off it seemed to attract me to her so much so that I could feel myself engrossed in her body. I wanted her more than anyone could imagine, yet I knew I could not, and I must wait.

Autumn came and it was back to school. This time, it was high school, a strange new world for me. It was a central high and the school was filled with strangers from miles around. The boys and girls were evaluating each other and within a few weeks most of the students were settled with their new choices. I did not pursue any new girlfriend because I was involved and the farmer where I worked paid me, as he put it, "when he had it," which was seldom.

The farmer and I agreed that he would pay me a dollar a day plus room and board. I was better off taking what I could get because the alternative was poverty and living at home. Therefore, I seldom had enough money to date girls. I didn't have a car for a while and I had to walk two miles each way to high school, rain or shine. One day, as I was on my way home from school, my lover friend was standing in the doorway all dressed up and as pretty as a picture. I wondered where she was going, she had just come from her doctor. I didn't realize what she was up to. She said, "I would like to see you this evening if you can make it." I said, "That would be okay."

I went out and tapped on the door as usual, and she opened the door and gave me a big hug. She seemed more affectionate than she had been for several weeks, but I did not expect anything but the usual kissing and tumbling. I said, "What is the good news?" I suspected she was going to tell me about an inheritance she had received from a trust fund her brother had set up for his appreciation for her staying home all those years and caring for their mother. I never thought for a minute that this was the night. I asked her what was the great news and was certain I knew the answer. She said, "Let's get into bed and I will tell you."

It was no problem getting nude and into the bed. I kissed her as usual and did the usual. What we had considered much pleasure and excitement by now had worn pretty thin. I said, "Come on tell me the good news." She said, "Brace yourself, I have seen my doctor today and he informed me that I cannot get pregnant."

A strange feeling came over me. I knew this was it, not later, now. I began to wonder how it would feel, would it meet with all my hopes and dreams? Just what would I want to do about the future? A thousand things went racing through my mind—not what I expected. All I could think was, WOW THIS IS IT, LET IT HAPPEN.

By now, we were in the right mood, in the right place, at the right time, and there was no barrier between us. It was so easy, so comforting, so exciting. It was more than I expected and time stood still for quite a while. Neither of us spoke a word. We just drifted into dreamland. What a beautiful experience. It was too much to comprehend. We spent about an hour just fulfilling for both of us a lifelong desire nature had provided.

It was difficult to leave her and go home. I said to myself, it happened so easily, it was so pleasant, so satisfying that it made everything else unimportant. I was living the life of financial frustration and the beauty of having just one something made life tolerable. It was not a substitute for success, but it encouraged me to press on, and time would bear fruition, if I kept trying and didn't give up. Happenstance had led me to the beginning of an understanding of what life is all about. It is what happens to you while you are letting opportunity talk to you.

Nothing much happened during the next two years, there was only farm work available and an occasional road building job. Poverty, it seemed, was going to doom the working class, only when one could find a job. Even those with good educations had a difficult time making enough to survive on. The farmer had asked me to stay and work on the farm, so at least I ate well and slept well. Of course, this was leading me to doomsville. I would grow up and become an old man with nothing. I had to plan to get away from the small town and get to someplace where I could get better vocational training and a meaningful job. No matter how hard I tried, all efforts led to nowhere. I would just have to wait for a miracle. I read every employment opportunity advertisement that I could find. No education. No trade. No job.

Another strange happening was taking place. On the farm where I worked, the farmer and his farm girl hired-hand would take the eggs and farm produce to the store on Saturday night and buy the things the farmer's wife would need for the next week. The farmer's wife and I would milk the cows, feed the animals and do the necessary farm chores twice a day, every day.

We had to get up at five o'clock in the morning in order to get all the work done before I would be able to go to school. That meant we would go to bed around nine p.m. in order to get enough sleep. It was a large farmhouse, with about six bedrooms, all on the second floor. It had a long hallway. My bedroom was across the hall from the farmer's wife's bedroom, but situated so that you could not see into the other bedroom. We left all the doors open so the heat and air could circulate.

As usual, on Saturday night the farmer and his girl went to the grocery store and the farmer's wife and I went to our respective bedrooms. We chatted across the hall and discussed the happenings of the day and plans for the next day, as we often did if we were going to do work out of the ordinary.

This Saturday night the farmer's wife said to me, "You are getting to be a big boy and you do not date any of the high school girls." She asked, "Aren't you interested in girls?" I said, "Sure I am interested in girls, especially one very nice farm girl, but your husband does not pay me, so how can I go out on a date without even enough money to buy her a soda? He buys the girls things, but says he has no money for me." She said she thought it was unusual that I did not show more interest in girls. I said, "I just got through telling you why."

I told her that I had feelings like everyone else and would like to date, but couldn't. I told her that I had never kissed a girl (which of course was a big fib). I told her that I would like to find out more about sex and things, but how could I?

I knew she was leading me on because I was aware that she and her husband didn't even talk to each other for months at a time. They hated each other and the farmer had his girls. He liked young girls and befriended them whenever he had the opportunity, which was quite often.

I asked her if I could kiss her, just to see how it felt. There was a long pause, and she said, "I'm an old woman, you wouldn't want to kiss me." I asked what difference it made, as if I didn't know. She was around fifty years young, with peaches and cream skin, very healthy and very likeable. I told her that I would like to do it once if she would be agreeable. She said, "It sounds silly that you should ask me. Why wouldn't you ask some of the young girls?" I told her I couldn't ask one of them, my face was flush just talking about it. She said, "Are you serious about kissing me?" I said, "Yes, could I come over and kiss you now?" She said, "If you really want to, come on over."

I went to her bedside, knelt down and put my arm over her and gave her a big sort of what I called a horse kiss. She said that it was okay, but I certainly needed to know how to kiss before I dated. She said, "You don't slobber, you do it gently, like this," and she really put the oomph in it. I played inexperienced. I said, "Well now, let me see if I can improve on my effort."

We spent about ten minutes practicing and I was getting in a worked up mood. I said to her, "Move over," and I put my hand onto that silk night gown again. She moved over and I got into bed with her. She said, "For a novice you move pretty fast." I agreed with her and apologized. Jokingly, I said, "It's your fault. If you weren't so sexy, I wouldn't have the problem."

She said I had better discontinue the lesson and go back to bed before they came home. I said, "Okay, but let me have one more of them there hi-potential kisses." She laughed and said, "Run before it's too late."

I said, "It's not too late. How about giving me a lesson

in real fun." She said, "Explain," so I put my hand on her breast and kissed her again. She squirmed. I asked her if I was bothering her, she said she was not made of stone. I said, "I am sorry to get you so roused up when all you wanted to do was be kind to me." I said that I would be pleased to subdue the feelings of both of us.

"Why don't we take a blanket and go out on to the porch, so we can see them coming if they come home early? If they show up we can pop back into bed and pretend we are asleep." She said, "You got me into this, so it's up to you to do something about it. The only thing is I warn you, if you go around bragging to your friends about what we are doing I will wring your neck." I said, "If your husband heard any news or rumors, he would kill us both." She said she knew what he was doing, so she didn't feel bad about what we were doing.

It was a night to remember. She really knew how to take care of me, and she did every time we had the opportunity, which was quite often. She admitted that she was planning to seduce me the first time she could. I told her that I was surprised, I thought she didn't like me. She said she hated me for making her wait so long. She really needed me and I was ignoring her. I told her it took a lot of courage to ask her because she was so nice and honest.

Now I had two old ladies to satisfy. It wasn't easy, but I managed. The only thing that bothered me was that I wondered if this was all there is to life. Where is it going to lead me? There must be a way of life besides illicit sexual encounters.

This was only the beginning, her sister lived on the other side of the mountain and she would have to walk past the farm fields where I worked. She would stop and pass the time of day by chatting and getting to know me better. Her husband had a weak back and couldn't do any hard work. She had become very muscular and was well built anyway. She was quite a bit younger than her sister and always in a pleasant mood when she stopped by to extend greetings and have a chat. I figured she was interested in me because she always stood close to me when she talked. In fact, she stood so close that it bothered me. I can't stand people who do that to me.

We would see each other once or twice a month in the farm field and she always appeared reluctant to get on her way. By now, I had lots of experience approaching girls in a way that would determine if they were interested in me and especially my body. I could sort of feel the mental waves flitting around. One day I said to her, "Does your husband's problem affect your sex life?" Her face became flushed and she said, "You are not backward about asking intimate questions." I apologized and told her that I was not well versed in just how to ask such a question. She accepted my apology and said, "The answer to your question is yes." Now I knew she was leading me on, so I asked her if there was anything I could do to help. She said, "As long as we are being frank and getting right to the point, there is something you can do if you think you are man enough." She said, "I probably am too much girl for you and I have been deprived for quite a while, so I might be too rough on you." I told her I would take my chances on that, when did she want to test me? She said, "How about right now?"

So we took the lap robe off the farm wagon and we tangled. She was right, she was rough and ready, and real good. In the wild range of excitement, I must have gone unconscious or something. I never occurred to me to ask if she could get pregnant because caution got lost in the mad fracas. Now I knew what she meant when she indicated that she might be too much girl for me.

Everything happened so fast and so easy that it took me a few days to retrace what had happened. She made a point of getting over to see me and talk about what we had done. She explained that was just the way she liked to do things. Don't play around, just don't do too much thinking. Make up your mind and get it done. That is what she had in mind about me and when the opportunity presented itself, she would not hesitate. In fact, she said that she had wanted me for over year, but hadn't found the right time before.

I asked her if she could get pregnant. All she explained was that she would take care of it, for me not to worry. Like a jerk, I didn't. We had quite a few good sessions later because we could meet in the farm woods halfway between her house and the farmhouse. It was so isolated that there was no danger. She could check to see if she was being followed and no one checked up on me.

Now, I had three older women that enjoyed the young boy. It bothered me that I was enjoying it even after realizing that I was not doing myself any good or doing anything to better my future. Strange, but I was always around whenever the opportunity presented itself. I had an insatiable desire for sex. I suppose it was because that was all I had, there was nothing else for me to do.

I wanted to do something of meaning, but how? My older brother was taking a course in electricity through a correspondence school and I had the opportunity to read a lot of the books. I got the idea that I could build a radio. There wasn't much to it in those days. It required a set of headphones, some copper wire, a crystal, a round oatmeal box, an "A" battery and a "B" battery, a switch and a lot of antenna wire (fifty to one hundred feet) mounted on the roof of the house and one end attached to the barn. The crystal was a piece of quartz. You wound the wire around the box for the coil and used a wire probe to see where the crystal was sensitive. After a few weeks of trying to find a spot on the crystal, I got a radio station which was six miles away. It was exciting to actually hear something that was being transmitted through the air. What was the world coming to, talking through the air without intermediate wires? Actually, the British gave it the name "wireless." It had a lot of wires to make it work. Terminology had its time and place and is unimportant to how well it performed. Quality was what counted.

I later built a one tube radio and subsequently built a four tube one. Now, I could receive New York City and listen to soaps, *The Lone Ranger*, *Green Hornet*, and operas. It took a lot of batteries so we had to ration the "on" time, then wait for the next day to do it again.

I tried to build an electric motor from thread spools and a lot of "pick-me-up" parts, but the wheel never turned.

HAPPENSTANCE shows its head again. There was a small time coal shipper that lived on the other side of the mountain. He was not rich, but had more money than the average person in the area. He also liked to boss everyone around and feel superior. He wasn't being obnoxious, it was just his personality. In fact, he was a very colorful character, as it was generally put. You couldn't hate him, but you kept at arms length from him. He was big and brazen, quite a fellow. He liked to do two things, drink booze and drink booze.

One day, he came over to the farm to get a few gallons of hard cider and someone told him about my radio. He said, "No one has a radio that good." He had heard good ones, but I should stop bragging and get with it, as he put it. I said, "It isn't hard to prove, come up to my workshop and listen for yourself." He tried to scare me by saying, "It better be good." I said, "Let's go," and he followed me. I tuned it in, and he said in his terms (censored), "You really did it or are you lying to me?" The farmer's wife verified that I had done it. He said," How long will it last?" I said "As long as you keep putting batteries into it."

I also told him that if I could afford a loud speaker it would be even better, everyone could listen. I told him they were expensive, probably two dollars. He gave me the money and said, "Go get one and hook it up." It took me an hour to go to town and buy one, but he waited for me and was surprised to hear the music so well. He said, "I will make a deal with you. I will trade you my 1917 Model T Ford for your radio." I figured I would be as bold as he was. I said, "Sometime when you are sober, you come over and we will talk." He said that he was not drunk, but I said, "You wouldn't know if you were drunk or sober. Come over with the title to the auto, and we will decide if you are sincere and if you are in a fit mood to trade." He agreed, took his prized loot, the hard cider, and left. As he was leaving he called me something under his breath, then went on his way.

One day, he came back with the title in his hand and said, "Now can we trade." I said, "You are serious?" He said, "I'm always serious." I said, "My radio is worth about fifteen dollars and your auto is worth several hundred." He said, "Not now, ya see Mom and the kids put a chain across the exit road from the garage, and I had to go around through the garden and up the railroad track to get out on to the highway. It didn't do too much damage on the way out, but the damn Sheriff tried to catch me before I could get back into the garage. Now it needs a bit more straightening and has a tire that blew, because it was poor quality." I said, "Sure, sure, always fault beyond yours." He said, "That is not the worst part. The Sheriff took my license to drive. He is an unreasonable so and so. I was not hurting anybody, and it is my auto. The Sheriff even had the audacity to tell me if he caught me driving until he returned my license, that he would lock me up as a hazard to humanity. (The unreasonable so and so)." I said, "Okay, you have a deal. Sign the title over to me and I will give you a bill of sale for the radio and install it for you." He said, "Good, we have a consummated deal, and I am sober."

Now the monkey was on my back. I had the title to an auto and the auto was in another town. It was in need of a few repairs and had a few flat tires that needed patching because they had taken a beating on the railroad track. It probably had enough gas in it to get it home. I had a valid driver's license, but the registration plates expired when the title was turned over to me. There was a Sheriff just waiting for the auto to come on the highway. What was worse, the Sheriff had a good reputation for always getting his man. It was no use trying to get by him.

My ever resourceful friend came to the rescue. "Let's take up a collection, get the license and share a ride to high school," he said. In the meantime, we would get the auto home by driving it through the woods and onto the farm where I worked. All we had to do was take down a few fences and we had it made. By having the auto home, we could straighten it out, repair the tires and be ready to go as soon as we had the ten dollars for the license plate. It took a few weeks to get the money together and we had a safe and comfortable way to get to school. In fact, I could get an extra hour of sleep because the two miles to school took only a few minutes in the car.

All went well, until one day one of the riders tried to crank the auto with the spark lever in the advanced position. The auto did what they called, "KICK," (reversed the crank with a quick motion) and he broke his arm. The auto did not have an electric starter. Most autos in those days did not have them. You engaged the crank and turned it until the motor started.

My friend told his father that a horse kicked him and his father asked, "Forrest's horse?" That was the end of the Ford. It had to go before anyone else got hurt, and there was no liability insurance on it. The boy's father paid the hospital bill for the broken arm. My neighbor heard that the auto was for sale and asked me how much I wanted for it.

I told him twenty-five dollars, he accepted the deal and gave me the money. I divided the ten dollars between all those who had donated to purchase the license. They were surprised, but I said, "It was not my money to keep." After that we were all walking again.

HAPPENSTANCE again: The farmer had a 1924 Chevrolet Coupe that he was not using. I told him that he owed me a lot of money and I would like him to sell me the Chevy for part of what he owed me. He said, "No way do you hold me up." I said, "I am not holding you up, you owe me wages, months past due." I offered him thirty-five dollars for the car. He just laughed. I said, "That is what you paid for it a year ago, and besides it needs the crankshaft bearings taken up. That is why you are not driving it." I told him I got the auto or he would talk to an attorney. He laughed and said, "I'm scared."

About a week later he got a summons to appear before the judge to answer charges of refusal to pay a workman's wages. He stopped laughing and signed the title over to me. I wrote to the judge and he withdrew the charges. I told the farmer I needed ten dollars for license plates. He didn't laugh. He just wrote me a check. This was the first time I had challenged a grown up, but it was because he made me angry. Besides, I caught him buying ice cream for young girls at the County Fair when he refused to give me even a dollar.

I now had an auto to drive to school and was able to pursue happiness. I was already pursuing more than I could handle, but I enjoyed a young girl's friendship for a change. It was quite different than that of a lady of fifty plus years.

HAPPENSTANCE WAS RIGHT ON TIME. I was getting disenchanted with the farmer and wanted to get away from his wife before he had his day in court. I read an ad in the local newspaper—"One farm hand wanted. Apply in person ready to go to work." The job was three miles from my parents' house, but the pay was two dollars a day and three meals, guaranteed pay every Saturday. I decided to take the job. I thought I would be able to hitch a ride once in a while.

My auto needed the bearings shimmed. My father agreed to help me repair it. We got the repair parts and started to fix it. It was a bigger job than we thought. I continued walking to and from work and we worked on the auto in my spare time. It was mostly down hill on the way home so that helped to make it possible to stay on the job at the farm.

After working many evenings and working on Sunday, we finally had the auto back together. We were relieved, until we discovered we had a "knock," and all our work was in vain. When we started it we had a hammer. It was worse than before. We joked about it and said it was the fault of the manual not us. I sold it to a garage mechanic and his manual must have been better than ours; it didn't knock at all, it purred like a kitten. We learned a good lesson. Do only what you have the ability to do, don't fake it.

I worked for the farmer for about two months and the

trek to and from work was getting to be too much for me. I decided to look for work closer home. The farmer said if I would stay on the job, I could sleep at the farmhouse and he would include a very good breakfast. I agreed and was back in business.

The farmer had a friend that came to dinner with his wife and two well behaved children of about eight years old. They were very friendly, but never discussed their vocation or employment. They were always well dressed and always socially proper. They had a late Model T Ford auto and always had it shined to perfection. I suspected he and the farmer had some kind of business going on between them. I found out years later that the farmer was into a lot of illegal things, such as making and selling moonshine whiskey and cattle rustling.

One morning after the family stayed overnight, I heard a lot of scuttling around and muffled voices which had become sort of unpleasant to listen to. Then the farmer came downstairs while I was eating my breakfast and said someone had stolen his wife's wedding ring and no one was leaving the house until whoever took it returned it to him. I said that I had never stolen anything in my life, and he could search me and my room if he cared to. He just got angrier and more boisterous and started to act like a madman. He demanded the ring be returned, right then, and said he would go to any length to get it back because there was more to it than monetary value; it was their wedding ring. As he became more violent, I said, "Do not look at me that way or try to harm me, because I am innocent and will defend myself, to death, if that is what it takes." He stopped looking at me and concentrated on his friend and his friend's wife.

The farmer's wife tried to calm her husband, but to no avail. She just kept on making delicious pancakes like none you have ever tasted. We all finished eating and the farmer's wife went to the laundry room to take care of the wash. She came into the kitchen and announced she had found the ring. She had put it into the robe she wore in the morning, had taken if off in order not to get it into the laundry water. She apologized for her short memory and the trouble she had caused. The farmer's friend just got in the Ford and went home. I stood up and said to the farmer, "I resign as of this minute. I am getting my few belongings and I too am going down the road before any more dangerous situations arise." He said he was sorry that he lost control of himself and thought his friend had stolen the ring because he was very poor and had a hard time surviving financially. The farmer said he was angry, especially because he always tried to help him.

I thought the farmer was trying to shift his shifty ways. I decided to stay because the food was good, the house was very comfortable to live in and on rainy days I did not have to do much work and got paid just the same.

There was a small shanty on the property which we called the Club House. We would spend evenings there with neighboring farm children and even the grown-ups would come over and play checkers and tell stories about what happened to them or gossip about what they had heard.

One day I said that the good food and exercise I was getting were doing me a lot of good. I could lift both back wheels of the ice wagon off the barn floor. The farmer said, "Do you know how much that wagon weighs?" I said, "It is very heavy, that is all I know." The farmer said, "I will bet you a month's pay that you cannot lift it. " I said, "This is a good time to prove it because there are lots of witnesses here to be the judges." The farmer said, "Let's go." I said I was ready.

We went to the barn, I put my back under the rear portion of the wagon, took hold of both rear wheels, picked it up about three inches off the floor, dropped it down, stuck out my hand and said. "You lost, I win, pay me." The farmer said he was only joking, I said, "We had a bet, pay up." He refused to pay and I said, "You will pay or pay dearly." He didn't look at all scared at the threat of a farmhand. He said, "Forget it." I wanted to resign, but there were only a few more weeks until school started, so I decided to continue working for those few days.

I was glad I had stayed because the farmer was very nice to me. His conscience must have been bothering him because the next Saturday evening when I told him I was going into town, he said, "It looks like it might rain, take my auto." It was a new Model A Ford with wire spoke wheels. Wow! Was I ever surprised and thrilled. I said, "Thank you very much, I will be very careful and drive slowly. Gosh will my friends be surprised to see me driving such a nice auto." When I got home, I wiped the dirt off the auto, especially the wire spokes. He was so nice to me that I could not believe a welsher could be that generous.

Finally, my employment time agreement had arrived. I packed my clothing and thanked them for giving me the job. The farmer handed me my pay, sixty dollars. I thanked him and said, "You really owe me another sixty dollars for the bet you made with me and lost." He smiled and said, "We have gotten along very well, it is better to forget some things and hope for a bright future. Look me up in the spring and we will probably be friends. It was good having you work for us."

When I went back to school, I told some of my friends what the farmer did, refusing to pay a gambling bet. They knew he made moonshine whiskey and sold it to a club in town. The whiskey would be put into a hollow tree down by the old mill, which was secluded. Hardly anybody ever went there and it was on his property. One of my friends said, "Let's empty out a couple of the bottles of whiskey and urinate into the bottles. Let him explain what happened to the club members. That will confuse them real good and the farmer will be hard pressed for an answer." We did that, and waited for a response.

The farmer waited in front of the high school and, needless to say, he was a very angry man. He said, "That was a very dirty trick to play on a person." I agreed, and reminded him that gamblers that welshed on bets usually died right there and then at the table. "If you have any plans of continuing the disagreement or doing harm to me, there are four of us and one of you. You really do not want to play against those odds, do you? I suggest you do what you told me to do, forget and hope for better days and never make a bet you do not or cannot afford. It could be injurious to your health."

That was the end of it. He never mentioned it again. About thirty years later, I was visiting the cemetery, checking up on the graves of my parents and brothers. I noticed his gravestone—big, bold and brazen. I did not believe the thought that came to my mind, and I said to my wife, "I have the fiendish thought of giving him one more portion of my brand of special moonshine." My wife said that she was ashamed of me, a grown man thinking like that. I really was not going to do it, but she thought I would.

HAPPENSTANCE struck again. The year I graduated from high school, I was looking for work by going from one farm to the other when I met a boy with whom I had gone to school. He was with a lady that was a stranger to me and much older than he was. He said hello and I greeted him. He said, "This is a friend of mine that is visiting the area." I said I had not met her before. She said that she had lived in the area as a youngster and as soon as she told me her mother's name, I said, "I know your mother, she has the only telephone and is very helpful when we have to contact anyone out of town." She said she was living in New York City and was glad to be able to get away from there and be able to walk in the country. I said, "I would like to go to New York sometime." She said, "How timely," because she and her girlfriend were in the process of setting up a luxury guest home for executives of the World's Fair and they could use a handyman that did not need a salary, someone that could work for room and board.

I thought to myself, big deal, I'm going to New York to be a handyman. Then I realized there was a possibility that I could go to night school and learn a trade, so the idea started to sound better. She asked me if I had any money. I told her I had about enough to get a train ticket and that was it. The clothes I was wearing were all I had, hardly appropriate for New York City. She said they would do for now and she could get me some better ones after they started to collect the money from the guests. She said that if I was sincere and interested, I could come out to her mother's house that evening and she would call her friend in New York and see if it would be agreeable with her.

It pleased her friend and she got the train tickets the next day. She made some sandwiches and picked some fruit so we would have a lunch on the train. Sandwiches and drinks on the train were very expensive, so we could have lunch without choking on the cost of it.

We had about an eight hour ride, so we had time to find out more about each other. My story was not very interesting because all I had to talk about was poverty and lack of the opportunity to get a better education and become gainfully employed. She said that there were plenty of possibilities, but it would be up to me to pursue them. As for her, she had been married to a very nice man who had a good business in New Jersey, just across the Hudson River from New York, but he was killed on a construction project and left her almost penniless. She had to work as a secretary and wait on tables in a restaurant in order to survive. She was now in her early fifties and was trying to establish a business that would give her some security.

We arrived in New York City early in the evening, got off the cross country train and went down a long flight of stairs to an underground train called a subway. A train came rushing into the station and we boarded it. It started with such rapid acceleration that the people who could not find seats and had to stand were really struggling to keep from falling. By the time everyone got settled, the train came to a stop and people scrambled into and out of the cars.

We rode for about fifteen minutes and I said, "How much further are we going?" She said, "A few more stops and we will be in a place called the Bronx." I said, "Why are we going there? I thought we were going to a place with a different name." She said, "Tonight we are going to stay at my friend's apartment and tomorrow we will go to the house that they rented. The furniture will be delivered and we will put it in place."

We got off the underground train and went up the stairs to the street level, where we went across the street and into a big apartment house. We got onto an elevator and went up about fifteen stories. She walked over to one of the doors, unlocked it and walked in. She said, "Welcome to New York."

It was all new to me. The bugs scrambled into the

cracks at the kitchen sink. I said, "What are they?" She said, "Roaches, everyone has them, they won't bite you, they are just a bit of a nuisance."

She opened some cans of food, made some hamburgers and we had a good dinner. We talked about the plans for setting up the guest home and how it would be taken care of. They were not planning to serve meals, so there would be a lot less work to do. I would spend lots of time cleaning, mowing the grass and doing the necessary every day chores.

It was approaching nine o'clock and I said I was accustomed to going to bed early because on the farm we had to get up early in order to milk the cows and do barn chores. She said, "Forget the farm, we probably won't get out of bed before seven or eight. We will be leading more of a night life. The movies, shows and entertainment are usually done in the evening and run until midnight in a lot of instances."

I asked her in which bedroom I was to sleep. She said, "Use the back room, it's small, but very comfortable."

I took a shower and got into bed. I heard her washing the dishes and puttering around in the kitchen, then she took a shower and came in to check up on me. I said I was doing fine, it was very nice. She said, "Move over." I didn't have much room to move because it was a single bed. She dropped her gown and got into bed with me.

I was really scared, I didn't know what she was up to. I said, "Would you mind telling me what is happening?" She said, "You are inexperienced, didn't you ever see a naked woman before?" I said, "I'm a kid and you are much older than me." She said, "Just take it easy, I won't hurt you, you will love every minute of it." I said I was not afraid to have sex, but I wanted to know what this arrangement was supposed to mean to me. She said her friend would be home the next day, she worked nights, she was a nurse.

The little girl from New England would be back from vacation in two weeks. "You are mine. I wanted to get to you before they did. I love a man and I am confident you will love taking care of me. I can't get pregnant, so there is no problem that way. In fact, being able to have you is part of the reason I was so quick to bring you to New York."

She convinced me to stay, she was very good and I couldn't argue with her. I told her she really scared the daylights out of me. She came onto me so fast that I didn't have time to get it all together and I felt trapped. I was concerned as to just what I had gotten into. She had a wonderful way of explaining what she wanted and did it frequently, almost every day. Her friends would go to work and as they say, we would go to town, our way. During the next two years we took care of the house and had a good time doing it. When the Fair was over, we were not able to get guests that could afford our prices. We had to make a quick decision. Our lease was up for renewal and unless we were lucky and could get new guests, we would have to vacate, but to where, and how. HAPPENSTANCE AGAIN saved us.

The realtors were doing their utmost to find guests for us. We ran an ad in the New York paper on our own. The phone rang one day and the person on the other end of the line asked if we took families. We asked how large the family was and inquired as to whether or not they were aware of the amount of rent we needed to stay in business. The man on the phone said it was a family of four—a husband, wife, a one-year-old child, and a nanny. We said that was alright if the price was satisfactory. He asked how much the rent was, and I told him five hundred and twenty-five dollars per month, payable in advance with a one month's rent security deposit. My heart jumped when he said that was more than he wanted to pay for four rooms.

And he was being fair, it was much too much, but we were caught in the middle, without enough income to pick up the difference. He asked if he could come over and examine the place and talk. He liked it and said four hundred was all he would pay. We partners had a quick talk and decided to accept his offer.

That left us with fifty dollars a month to live on, buy food, etc. We all agreed to chip in and make a go of it. The lady from my home town said she would stay home and keep things under control and we three others could contribute. It worked out well, I got a job as a grocery store clerk at twenty dollars a week. Between us we made up the one hundred and twenty-five dollars per month. We had another year that we could stay in the house, eat and sleep, which was a lot for three limited income people.

Toward the end of the fiscal year we tried again to find a guest, but nothing happened. We did not have high hopes because we knew we were operating at luxury price levels and the handwriting was on the wall. We were not going to be able to make it. I decided to go back to the farm country and do the best I could—survive. The nurse decided to get a low cost apartment and stay in New York. The lady from my home town decided to go to a Midwestern town where she had relatives and try to find work. The little girl from New England said her only option was to go back home and find a position where she could survive on a secretary's salary. "HAPPENSTANCE, where are you? I need you."

I thought of everything from A to Z, as they say. Then I got the brilliant brainstorm. I would ask the little girl to marry me. I reasoned that if we combined our income, we could afford a one bedroom apartment and feed ourselves. I could go to night vocational school and better myself. One evening, I asked the little girl if she would meet me at a local sandwich shop. I had a proposal to offer her. She said, "Why can't we talk right here and now?" I said I wanted privacy and time to present my plan. She agreed to meet with me and we sat down, ordered sandwiches and coffee. I looked right at her and said, "Let's get married and make a go of it together."

She looked at me as if I had hit her with a baseball bat. She was an angry girl, yes angrier than that. She said, "You have a nerve to ask me to marry you. My God, you are bold and brazen aren't you? I lived in the same house with you for three years and you didn't even say hello or good-bye. In fact, you didn't care anything about me. In fact, I am of the opinion you don't like me at all. I think you are using me for your own convenience."

I told her that I deserved to be told off, but to think about it. "It is an expediency to survival and love will find a way." I told her that I knew she was a good person, struggling to get along and I would be honest, trustworthy, and do everything to try to improve myself for our benefit.

She got up, walked out of the restaurant and went home to her room. I knocked on her door because I heard her crying. I told her I was sorry and apologized for my clumsy proposal, but I was really worried about her. (I should have told her that I wanted to get away from my sexual partner.)

The next morning, she came down to breakfast. We were the only ones in the breakfast room. I thought it better if I kept my mouth shut and not exacerbate the problem that I had started. She just sat looking at me for about five minutes and then she said, "I spent all night thinking over what you said." In fact she had decided not to go to her job that day. Her eyes were red. She said, "If there was any other way of putting it I wouldn't be distraught. You will be surprised; I have decided to go along with your stupid proposal, only because I have no other choice. You go find an apartment that we can afford and I will call my father and mother and try to explain to them what we were up to. You might as well know right now, I am eleven years older than you." I said it did not matter to me at all. Many people marry with age differences.

I found an apartment in a two story house on the second floor. It was near the transit station, so we had little trouble getting to work. We told the furniture dealer of our predicament. He was a very nice man and said, "Take enough furniture for your needs. It is a gift from me to you. You took good care of the furniture during your lease with the store." I didn't even know that my partners had acquired the furniture on a lease purchase plan. The stipulation was, if the business of the guest house failed, he would pick up the furniture and tear up the contract; in fact, that was what he was doing that week. What a break! I had visions of eating off cardboard boxes and sleeping on the floor for a while.

We moved the furniture into the apartment. The little girl advised me of a problem. I was not permitted to sleep there until we were married. She said she would sleep there, and I could do whatever I cared to, but I would not sleep there. I went looking for a furnished room for a few weeks. Not too far from the apartment, there was an old cardboard sign in the window—"Furnished Room for Rent." I went over and knocked on the door. The bell didn't work. The big, old, unkempt man showed me the room. "Five dollars a week, in advance," he said. I said I would take it and handed him five dollars. He looked at the five dollars and said in a gruff voice, "Five more please, security deposit. You will get it back if I decide to return it when you check out." I gave him another five, which was about all I had and he handed me a key and laid the house rules down to me. "You break them, I kick you out. The bath is down the hall—you use it, you clean it. Don't leave your dirt for someone else to clean up after you. Enjoy your stay."

After he left the room, I took a look at the bed. I had seen sway back horses, but this bed topped them all. If you attempted to lie on your stomach you would break your back. I actually took the mattress off the bed, laid it on the floor, then in the morning I put it back on the bed. The nice part of it was the room was clean.

I went to the apartment the next evening after work to help get things put into place. I told the little girl about the awful bed. She said, "No excuses, until we are married you can have all the excuses you want to, but you will not sleep here. I am an honest, upright living Christian girl and we are going to keep it that way. I feel sorry for you, but I will not violate my principles for you or anyone else."

We expedited the process of getting married and I was one very glad boy to get out of that sway bed. He gave me back my five dollar deposit because I "toed the mark" as he put it.

All was quiet and peaceful, things were running smoothly. We saved up a hundred dollars and bought an old auto so we could get out of town and see some of the country.

HAPPENSTANCE. Yep, right on time.

About two thirty in the morning our bedroom was lit up by a bright light. I wondered what was taking place. I went over to the window and a police car was shining the light onto the house. The policeman said, "Are you the owner of a Pontiac Sedan that is parked on the side street lot near to Queens Boulevard?" I said, "Yes, what am I being arrested for, what have I done wrong?" He said, "You have done nothing wrong, we caught two boys stealing the tires and wheels off your car. We have the boys here in the police car and your tires in our trunk, we need you to come with us to the police department to sign a complaint." I said I would be right down.

We went to the precinct headquarters and did all we had to do and they locked the boys up and drove me home. The policeman said I would have to leave the tires and wheels at the property clerk's building until the trial and sentencing. I said, "No problem." I thanked them and went to bed.

The trial date was set and the boys appeared before a man I called "Hangman Harry." He had no use for thieves. The boy's mother asked the judge for clemency. He growled back at her. "Clemency! Lady, they should be hung, they are not better than horse thieves, I'll tell you right now they are going to the State Workhouse for at least two years. We have to get their kind off the street." I said, "Your Honor, I also would like to plead for a lessor sentence for the boys, if it is their first offense." The judge said, "No way, they must be punished."

Then he asked, "Where do you boys work?" They said, "In a factory." The judge asked them how much money they earned and the boys said, "Forty dollars a week." The judge said, "Each of you makes forty dollars a week and you are out in the night stealing? You don't make sense. Who are you working for?" The boys refused to tell. The judge said, "We will find out, and if you lie to me or cover for someone, I will extend your sentences." The boys said they would be killed if they talked.

When I heard the boys were earning forty dollars a week each, I remembered the name of the company, and on my first day off from work I went to the factory and applied for a job. The personnel manager asked me what kind of work I could do. I said, "Anything that you want to

44

assign me, I will do it." He said, "You have no trade, all I can give you is a bench hand's job." Fifty-five cents per hour. Now it was time to make a decision. Fifty-five times forty is twenty-two. Whatever happened to forty? What should I do? I decided to accept it because there was opportunity there, where there was almost none at the grocery store.

In my darkest moment of wondering if I had done the right thing, the personnel manager asked me if I could work overtime. I was afraid to answer because at the store I had worked at least ten hours a week overtime without getting paid for it. If you didn't stay at the store after hours and help clean up, you got fired. So I told the personnel manager the store's policy. "Here we pay time and a half for the first two hours overtime and double time after that." Wow! What a difference. I went home a happy boy. The job in the factory worked out very well. I was committed to doing as I promised and never refused to do anything.

I enjoyed wiring and soldering. At last I was doing something that meant something. The thing that I was putting together would make a machine run; therefore, it was very important to make certain that I did the work to perfection. The machinery was to be used for the war effort and most of it was complex, so one had to be sure of what he was doing.

One of the machines was driven by direct current electricity. If the wires were put into the wrong terminal, the wires would heat up so badly that the insulation would get very thin and cause a short circuit, even if the polarity was corrected. The wires that were damaged had to be replaced and it was dirty work and very costly. I had studied my brother's home study books about how to make a small, low current generator. I scrounged up some old generator parts and built the device and used it to check the wiring before it was subjected to full power. All the wires were in their place and you put it onto the tester, a red light would come on and it was easy to correct the wiring and then put it onto full power, and nothing would be damaged.

One day the foreman asked me what that contraption was. I explained it to him and he was pleased. About that time the head tester came hurrying to the place where I was showing the foreman how it worked. The foreman asked him if it was as good as I said it was. He agreed, but made the statement, "If this fellow is going to build test equipment, perhaps you don't need me." The foreman said he would consider what the tester said. I said, "Now look fellows, I don't want to cause any trouble, I do not like pulling those burned wires out and putting in new ones." The tester did not resign and the foreman did not fire him. I must say, there was no love lost between me and the tester.

A week later the Vice President in charge of manufacturing was in the factory and the foreman told him what I had done. He suggested the foreman promote me to a straw boss. This was not assistant foreman, just a fellow that helped employees with problems and sort of looked out for anything that would keep the job from running smoothly. I was given a fifteen cent per hour increase in my pay. Seventy cents per hour times forty was twenty-eight dollars per week—a far cry from forty. But there was plenty of overtime, so I was doing alright and moving along in the right direction. I was given quite a few rapid increases in salary because the boss could see I was working in the interest of the company.

The time finally arrived when the contract for the machines came to an end. The order was completed and there was no more work for me. Lots of the people were dismissed with thanks for their loyal service. Naturally I was at my wit's end as to what to do. I had little experience except in building the machines. In fact, I was scared. What would I do? What would my wife think when I told her that I was laid off. The thought occurred to me to ask the Personnel Manager if there was absolutely anything I could do to keep some sort of a job with the company. He said that because of my loyalty to the company, he would look around and try to place me somewhere. He asked me to report back to the factory in a few days and he would do his utmost, but he said not to bank on it. It sounded like a brush-off to me, but I did as he asked.

I went back to the factory and he told me he had a job in the steel casting yard, unloading steel from railroad cars. He said, "It's dirty work and it's cold out there in the yard." The job was also for less money than I had been getting. I surprised him when I said, "I'll take it."

He was right, it was dirty and cold, but he had forgotten to mention the word "dangerous." One day the steel chain on the overhead crane broke and steel beams went flying all over the place. One of the workmen missed being killed by inches. I took extra precautions every minute and went looking for another job at every opportunity. A lot of other former employees were looking too. Everywhere I went I was told my buddies had already been there. There were no jobs available. I stuck it out on the dirty job for several weeks.

One day the Personnel Manager said he had a better job for me. It was inside of the factory and involved much more money. I was to be a tool inspector. It involved checking all the machine tools for damage and dullness after each time they were used. If they needed repair, I would issue a repair order and send them for repair. If they were OK, I was to put them into the bin where they were stored. I was also to keep records of who was using the tools.

I had this job for about four months and one day one of the bean counters, as they were called, discovered I was getting too much money to do that job. He insisted that my salary be reduced immediately. I think this sort of annoyed the Personnel Manager because he said to the efficiency man, "You have no heart." This was my first experience with factory politics at work.

The Personnel Manager made up his mind that he would get the better of the bean counter. He had an opening in the Inspection Department for a Purchased Material Inspector. I told the Personnel Manager that I thought the job was beyond my capabilities. It required reading blueprints and I did not have too much experience in that field. He said, "Get going and get experience, do whatever is necessary to learn." I took the job and signed up for a night school course at the Vocational School. That way, when I needed help, I could go to the instructor and get the necessary help. It worked out very well. The Personnel Manager said, "If you don't know, don't let anyone know it. Get help and no one will ever know."

I found out later that he too was underpaid in accord with what other managers in the area were getting. That is why he had compassion for me, a young fellow trying to hang onto a job because it was a job and there were no other jobs to be found.

One day the Personnel Manager and the bean counter had a head to head showdown discussion over his wages. The bean counter absolutely refused to give him an increase in salary, so the Personnel Manager called the Plant Manager, told him of the encounter and demanded more money, or else. This was a fatal mistake. The Plant Manager was a person who would listen to reason, but no one ever got away with that "more or else" bit. The Plant

Manager said he would let him know right after lunch. As promised, the Plant Manager called him and said he would accept his resignation with the usual "regrets," effective immediately. Surprise!

The Plant Manager's personal secretary, his very valuable assistant, informed him that she too was resigning, immediately, and she and the Personnel Manager (who were both unmarried) were sweethearts and she was going with her lover. The Plant Manager would not be intimidated by them and he wished them Godspeed and much happiness. They cleaned out their desks and departed.

One day the Union representatives ganged up on the Plant Manager and burst into his office. He, being a very educated man, just sat there shaking his head and saying, "I DON'T BELIEVE IT, I DON'T BELIEVE IT," repeating the phrase several more times to himself. Finally the Union leader said, "What don't you believe?" He replied, "I don't believe the Personnel Manager hired a mob." The Plant Manager said he would talk to them, one at a time, but he would not try to talk to a mob. It worked. They dispersed and the Union leader stated what he wanted in the form of a demand, not a request. The Plant Manager told him that demands are HARSH words and said he would like the Union leader's demands to be put in as a request, that way he would be able to consider the answer in a more dignified frame of mind. The Union leader apologized. They talked it over and the problem was resolved without arbitration. They all became well aware of the fact that Bill was firm, fair, and quick to fire. He took no nonsense from anyone. That is why I liked working there. I always knew I could have my day in court, as the old saying goes.

One day the Plant Manager's new company automobile

was delivered to the Incoming Inspector of Purchase Materials. I was given the invoice along with other materials delivered by truck. The Plant Manager called me and asked me to have the auto driven to the entrance to his office. I informed him that the auto had just been delivered and I had the paper to inspect it. He said he wanted to go for lunch. I informed him that I would put it on a priority list of items to be inspected. When and if it was as per invoice, I would have it taken to where he wanted it. He said, "I don't think you heard me, I want to go to lunch." I said, "Yes sir, I will do it next and accept or reject it." I took the invoice and quickly checked everything on the order and made sure everything was on the auto and working. It took about five minutes to perform the inspection. It was as per order and I asked the chauffeur to take it to the designated place. In the meantime, I called the Manager and said the auto was as per order, everything on it worked as it should. He thanked me and hung up the phone. I expected him to be angry with me, but I suppose he decided it was better to let me do the job the company was paying me to do.

One time there was a special shaft purchased to be inserted, freeze fit, on a large gear. I would guess the shaft and gear were worth several thousand dollars and had to be machined to a thousandth of an inch specifications. I took special care to make certain the shaft was as per order to the extent of noting the room temperature at the time I verified the measurements. On a shaft that diameter the room temperature could vary it more than one ten thousandths of an inch. They ordered the dry ice and had everything in place to assemble the gear and shaft. They would not go together. The procedure was to freeze the shaft and heat the gear so when the two items were at the same temperature the gear and shaft would be forever one piece. When the effort to assemble it failed, everyone accused me of not inspecting the shaft. They sent for the Chief Inspector, the Chief Engineer, and the Plant Superintendent. Even the Plant Manager was brought into the assembly area to listen to what was transpiring. The Plant Manager quietly said to me, "Did you inspect the shaft and was it machined to the specification?" I assured him that I had even checked the room temperature at the time I measured it. I said, "Just one moment. I will go to the vault where the reports are kept and return with the invoice copy with all the facts and figures on it." Some of the shop people still said it was my fault. The Plant Manager asked me if I could shed any light on why it did not go together. I said, "Let me have a look at the gear work order so that I can determine if the machining specifications were correct for the assembly." When the work order was delivered to me, I looked it over and I found that the final bore was to be done in the shop at this location, rather than where it was cast. They machined the gear and put it together. After that, none of my factory enemies ever tried to accuse me of not doing my job. The next week I noticed quite a large increase in my salary by order of the Chief Inspector.

For the next four years everything ran smoothly. One morning the Superintendent called me into his office. The Chief Inspector, Chief Engineer, Plant Manager and the Personnel Manager were all seated around the conference table. The Plant Manager asked me how I would like to leave my duties as an inspector. I replied that if it was for something I had done wrong, if it was a voluntary resignation, I would not be too happy about it. I asked, "What is the problem?" They all looked at me and I was puzzled as to what was going on. They were initiating me into the executive division. When I was about ready to think I was being let go, the Plant Manager said, "You have been inspecting all that material for the new Controller Department. We have been looking for someone to take charge of that division and make a go of it." I said, "Come on fellows, don't do this to me, you know a job like that is over my head. You have a lot of well qualified men that can run that operation. Why pick on me?" The Superintendent said, "It's a thirty dollar per week increase in your pay, starting today." I said, "That may be well and good, but you know I cannot do that job well. Please do not do this to me." The Plant Manager said, "Stop whimpering and go up to our other plant and get some idea of how it's done." I said, "Thanks for your confidence in me," and walked out of their office one scared fellow. Hiring and supervising hundreds of people! I felt like running away, but said to myself, "Give it a try. You can't fail unless you try. This is your big opportunity, don't blow it."

I returned from the other factory within a few days and the Plant Manager asked me what I was doing there. He said I was supposed to be at the other factory. I told him I had seen all I cared to see of the way they were producing the units. In my opinion, they were too careless and made too many mistakes. They seemed to be having a lot of trouble getting the units to function properly. He said, "Start hiring the people you need to manufacture the units." WOW! Hire a couple of hundred people for whom I would be responsible!

I placed an advertisement in the newspaper and the applicants were to report to the Personnel Department and if they were qualified, Personnel would send them to me for my decision, whether I accepted or rejected them. Girls were easier to hire, they seemed more eager to get a job. Men were more selective about whether or not they wanted the job. Opening day came and everything was in place. I started the relay assembly lines, the metal frame assemblers were getting their part done and I was busy explaining circuitry to the new wiring. Most of the wiremen were very experienced and all they needed were the schematics (wiring diagrams). Everything ran well, without much difficulty. I was surprised. It now occurred to me that it would be a snap if I kept a close watch on everything. I was also surprised that the employees didn't mind me looking over their shoulders. In fact they were pleased that I was friendly and interested in how well they were doing the work. Within a short time we became one big happy family. I was afraid it would get too friendly.

We had eight good years of producing a quality product. One day the Vice President in charge of manufacturing came into the department and sort of smiled and said, "You have a good thing going here! You design the units, build them, test them, check them for quality and appearance, and ship them. Nobody is checking on you." I said, "Yes there is someone checking on me, the field assemblers and installers." I asked if there were any field complaints? He said, "Very few." I asked what the problem was and he said the company structure was not set up that way. The engineers designed the units, the Manufacturing Department built them, the Testing Department tested them, Quality Control made certain that they were as per specifications and the work was done well. I said, "I don't want to oppose your procedures, but your way makes it easy for the blame game to function when things go wrong." He said he agreed with me and said to continue as I had been doing. "As long as you are in charge," he said, "there is very little to worry about." I was not in charge much longer.

After ten years, the company decided to move the

production to the Midwest where it would be in the center of its market. The salary increase they offered me to relocated was not worth all that was involved. They offered me an Assistant Supervisor's job in Architectural Products without reducing my pay. I was glad they did not terminate me for declining the offer to transfer.

Their selection for a Supervisor was a pitiful one. They selected one of my wiremen that knew nothing about how the units were designed or operated. All he knew how to do was to follow the wiring charts. These were very complex, automatic electrically controlled machines. You guessed it, he was a first cousin of one of the big boys. I knew disaster was only weeks away.

About two months later the company bought an electronics factory nearby. They were breaking into solid state controls and electronic switching. I heard about the purchase, but paid no attention to it because I was confident they would be able to get a lot of experienced employees from the company they had acquired. Again they went into it without my help. They built four of the very complex units, put them to the test and the units did everything except explode. The V.P. came running and told me to get over there and straighten the units out. He said, "Go right now and speed it up. Someone in the Scheduling Department has assigned units that were part of a penalty contract." I had two weeks to do four weeks' work. The units were so fouled up, I could not get them to function. I said I would have to remove every wire and rewire all four of them. The V.P. said, "Just do it. Spare no expense to have them on the shipping platform on the required date."

I put on three shifts and virtually stayed in the factory to insure nothing would go wrong. The day they were to be shipped they were crated and ready to go. The V.P. was one happy fellow. He gave me a substantial increase in salary and assigned me to take charge of everything in the new factory. I balked at his offer. I said, "What about the present set up?" He said, "Alright, I see what you mean, but anything you decide to do to keep things moving, no one will interfere with you. All I want you to do is be certain that you send a copy of everything you do to my office, signed by you and dated." The upper management asked, "Why do we need King Tut to assist with the work?" The worst part was that they found out about the increase in salary I had been given. The Plant Manager said I was getting more money than their superintendent. I told him, "I didn't ask for this assignment, in fact, when the V.P. told me the job was permanent, I said, 'Don't I have a choice?' He said, 'You sure do. Take it or leave.'" He showed no mercy to me. He needed me and that settled the order. After a few weeks we all felt differently toward each other and peace and harmony reigned.

Then the V.P. threw the monkey wrench into the calm. He started a Research and Development Division and sort of inferred that I was to think up the new ideas and put them together. Again, there was dissension. I was surprised at the V.P.'s decision. He even went so far as to pay for a college semester in research and development for me and the head of the Research Department. (He was a brilliant man, a consultant to the X15 rocket and projects of that magnitude.) I couldn't even begin to consider myself in his class. I was not even good enough to be a novice in the field. However, we worked well together and he was most considerate of the company's decision. We designed and built quite a lot of special equipment for the Army and Navy. We also designed products for other companies. The company seemed to have a priority on bidding for contracts. I am confident it was because we produced a quality product, on schedule, at a fair price. It looked like I would have a job as long as I wanted it.

One day a group of men walked into the factory and identified themselves as purchasers of the company. The President of that company informed me that he was transferring the entire division to the Midwest and because I did not have an engineering degree he would have to offer me a menial job at about half the pay I was receiving as Supervisor at the factory. I told him I could not afford to accept a salary at less than I was receiving. He said that was his best offer. I told him I would look for employment elsewhere. Due to the complexity of all the projects, he asked me how long I would stay to help with the closing of the division. I told him I would stay as long as he didn't tamper with the cash register, meaning as long as he didn't reduce my pay. He said, "Let's make a termination date of three months from now." I agreed and thanked him for the consideration. I really should have kicked him because he knew he was using me.

I thought that with twenty-one years of manufacturing experience it would be easy to obtain a very good job, possibly closer to home. I soon found out that without a degree, I was not going to get a very well paying job. After six weeks of filing resumes, going for interviews, and hearing "Don't call us, we will call you if we decide to hire you," I was finally being considered for a position as Assistant Plant Manager at a small ornamental steel fabricating company at a pay that I could survive on, and the growth potential was very good. The owner of the company was satisfied with my background, especially the architectural experience I had, even if it was only for a limited number of years. He said he would verify my application and let me know when to start to work.

About three weeks went by and I did not hear from

him. I decided to go to his factory and check up on the possible employment. He said that he doubted if I had ever worked for the company, especially for twenty-one years. He said he had called the company and the secretary in Personnel had no record of me. She was one of the new buyer's employees and my records had been sent to the company's headquarters in New York so they could get my pension papers filed and send out my severance pay. I told the owner of the factory I would bring him proof of all the projects that I had initiated, my safety record certificates and my budget and cost control records. He said he didn't want anyone working for him that didn't tell it straight. I said I could verify every word I had told him. He said I must have made little impression on the company if they did not remember my being there for such a long time. I tried to explain, but he said I was wasting my time. I was getting a lesson in the way business was mismanaged. Twenty-one years of faithful service were distorted by a stupid secretary that should have known what to do. I thought HAPPENSTANCE also had forsaken me. Not so.

The best thing that ever happened to me was that I did not get that job. I trotted the streets for about a month and there was no hope of getting a good job. I was the fair haired boy that had been passed by, through the evolution of progress. I realized that I would have to find another type of employment. I began to inquire about anything that I thought I could do. The result was about the same. It looked like I would have to sell my house, go back to the hills and become a gentleman farmer. I had enough money to pay cash for a farm and stock it. I was going to hire a farm boy and a farm maid to do the work. We could take it easy and make a living.

One day I noticed an advertisement for a real estate

salesman that said an attorney/real estate broker would train salespeople and help them get the state license required. I called the broker. He asked me a lot of questions and determined that it was a marginal risk betting on my becoming a successful salesman. I said I had a lot to offer because I was ambitious, and because I had a habit of eating, I needed a job. He said to come down and we would talk some more. We got along quite well after we found out what each of us could do for the other. The job was strictly commission, no salary. I would go through six weeks of schooling and then take the state exam to qualify for the license. I paid attention to every word he said because he was a successful attorney and broker. I took the test and passed. Now I was a real estate salesman.

I had to file an estimated income tax and pay the quarterly amount due. My automobile was very old, but I shined it up, took the junk out of it, and—oh yes—it needed gasoline, oil and tires, which had to be paid for in advance. Taking clients to lunch, hoping they would buy something, driving all over town looking for listings, making telephone calls and other expenses without any money coming in made me wonder if I was "Hopeful Harry," as the saying goes.

After the first year I had made fourteen small sales that did not cover all my living and business expenses. I didn't have much choice but to try it for at least another year.

HAPPENSTANCE smiled again. I saw an advertisement in the paper for a shopping center site for sale—one hundred thousand dollars. I said to myself, "If I can list that and then sell it, at ten percent commission of the selling price, after I split the commission with the broker, I will get 5,000 dollars." I rehearsed my sales pitch a couple of times because I knew I was going BIG TIME. I called the owner and asked him if I could come to his office and discuss selling the property. He said I could come see the property, but he would not give me an exclusive listing on it because there were brokers involved. I decided not to take no for an answer if I was going to be a success.

I drove to his office, which was about thirty miles away, and parked my junker down the street, went in to his office, and greeted him with a hearty handshake. What he did not know was that I was shaking inside and a little bit insecure about meeting a big property investor. He had a beautiful office building, and the entrance was impressive, for it had a running waterfall.

I got right down to business by asking him for a copy of the survey and type of municipal zoning. I asked about utilities available and the population of the area, as well as what competition was involved and the terms of the sale. I inquired as to whether or not they wanted to hold a mortgage and how soon they wanted to give over possession of the property. He said, "You are aggressive, you really want to know a lot about the property and area." I said, "My clients will want to know and I will be prepared to tell them." I could see he was impressed and he was shuffling in his chair.

I changed the subject by asking him if he owned the ambulance parked outside the front door. He told me he was the County Coroner and also owned a funeral home. I said I was impressed. He remarked that I must have had a lot of management experience. I said I had twenty-one years of it with a large company and told him the short form of the gory details. Then I said, "Let's get back to the shopping center."

He said that he could not give me an exclusive because of reasons he had already explained. I told him my broker would not let me try to sell it without brokerage protection.

He said he would give me a brokerage protection letter stating that if we sold the property he would pay us five percent commission based on the selling price. He said he doubted if we had buyers for that kind of property. I said, "We sure do, we are near to the airport and the cross country railroad where a lot of the big buyers come to the area via those facilities." I almost had to laugh at my being able to come up with con merchant answers.

He said the truth of the matter was that the company was in the red and going broke, that was why he wanted to sell the shopping center land, in order to get money which was sorely needed. He said he also owned a large construction company that built residential houses; it also was in poor straits. I said, "I cannot believe you are not doing well with all the construction equipment, trucks and the like sitting around." He said, "That is the problem, they are sitting when they should be active." I asked him what was the reason, and he told me it was due to the lack of a good person to generate sales. I said, "You have seventeen salespersons' licenses hanging on the wall. Where are they?" He said, "They had part-time jobs and tried to sell real estate in their spare time." I told him that would never work, selling was a full-time job and involved extra hours if you were to be successful. Again, I said to myself, "Listen to the neophyte talking."

I must have impressed him very much. He asked me to become General Manager of the company and get it rolling. I asked how he could pay me if there was no money in the till. He said he would figure out some way. I told him it is impossible to pay if you don't have it and I had only a small amount of cash in reserve. I would have to see some light at the end of the tunnel, financially. I decided to make him an offer. I would manage the company on a strictly commission basis. Forty percent of the total on everything I sold and a five percent share of each salesman's commission. In return to the sales people I would assist them and make sure they were selling, not entertaining the prospects.

Most sales persons believed if they wined and dined the prospects, they would buy. That is not true. If the buyer is sincere and you have the merchandise to offer them, there is no time for kidding yourself. Present the property and ask them to make an offer, that is the way to determine if you have a buyer or a looker. Show the prospect everything in the category in which he is interested and if he does not make an offer, explain that this is all you have to show him and bid him a handshake good-bye. If he says he will think about it, tell him when he decides to let you know. Don't call him, he will just waste another day for you.

The owner said, "When can you start work?" I said "Tomorrow." I told him there was one other matter we had not discussed, I wanted complete control over everything, including him. He was shocked, he said it was not proper for the C.E.O. to have authority over the owner. I said I didn't have time to get involved in split decisions, it was a waste of time. If he didn't like what I was doing, it was his company, he could tell me to get lost. He was upset, but he said, "I see what you mean. We will do it your way." He smiled and said I would not have a problem supervising the employees. I assured him I followed the rules. He said, "You are here to do the job you were hired to do and if you don't want to do it I will accept your resignation."

I issued a bulletin and posted it on the bulletin board stating that any salesperson that wanted to work full-time was to report to my office on Monday morning at nine o'clock. All other licenses papering the walls would be returned to the Real Estate Commission, which meant the persons to whom they belonged were no longer employed at the company. They were free to go elsewhere, but resolve it with the License Bureau. The owner said, "You can't do that. Most of these people are my relatives." I asked him how many deadbeats he could afford to have hanging around running up expenses and producing very little. He said he would send them to me if they got upset over the decision. I said, "That is the thing to do. It won't bother me a bit."

We started an extensive advertising campaign and rented a highway billboard. We made very expensive realty signs and everyone was told to somehow get permission to put a sign onto the property, exclusive listing or open listing. We created quite a furor in the town. A lot of people came in and asked what was happening. We told them that the large shopping center and a few industrial things were just the beginning of rapid area growth. They believed us and success was creating success. I cleaned the three model homes and issued a statement that anyone caught in any of the model homes after dark would be arrested and locked up. I had made arrangements with the State Police to do so. One fellow had quite a lot of stock in the company and said, "Surely the order doesn't include me." I said, "Think about it before you violate my order. There are no exceptions." He was one of the people that was misusing the model homes. He did not challenge me because he was a married man and thought better of it to try me.

Things began to move along, people were coming into our office and ordering homes to be built and the new personnel were converting new home buyers into resale buyers, which gave us immediate cash. We opened a home repair division and that was a good money maker from the start. We were in a position to do a mole hill or a mountain of business. We had the equipment and the know-how.

One day a franchise owner came into the office and asked if we could move two houses and complete a store for him within thirty days under penalty contract, meaning if we did not have the store building ready for occupancy within that time he could bill us for everyday we were late in completing it. I said, "Just a minute." I pressed the button on my two way radio and said, "Sam, where are you?" He said he was enroute to a job site. I asked, "Can you come to the office right away?" He was there in a few minutes and we discussed the plans and assured him we could do the job very easily. He said he believed me because we were so organized. Good thing he didn't know the whole truth, but we usually managed to keep things on track. This was a break for us, and we erected a big sign saying the project was being built by our company. It was a ground breaker. Other businesses followed by having their buildings built by us.

One big item I overlooked was that we were over saturating the area with one family homes. One day I was faced with the problem of what to do with fourteen houses that were not selling. Another builder had come into the area and built a small house on a slab (no basement). People bought them because they could afford them easier than our houses. We spent a lot of money on advertising and reduced the price to almost no profit. They finally sold and we went into commercial building and kept the real estate business. We built custom homes on a prepaid basis, that way we could not lose money on them.

I was making a lot of commission money, and the second year I was able to buy a year-old model new Cadillac and pay all my living expenses. The third year I bought a new airplane and paid cash for it. I started a flying club and taught students to fly. The fourth year I bought another smaller airplane called a commuter. It was good for short hops and cut down on a lot of driving.

It seems like every time things go well something happens to distort it. My wife developed Lobar Pneumonia and died within three days. The doctor didn't think she was in any danger. He gave her a prescription and said he would see her on Friday. She died on Wednesday, before Friday. What a shock! It was just like pulling the curtain down on a thirty year happy marriage, just when we could afford to enjoy life. I was a walking zombie. Nothing seemed to make sense, she couldn't be gone. Only those that suffer such a loss can understand the feeling. I would think of things to talk to her about when I got home, before the reality set in that she was not there. I wouldn't draw a contract for quite sometime. I just was not with it.

One day the minister of the church asked me if I could stay after church. He wanted to talk to me. He told me to come out of it. I was living with a memory that was going to kill me. He said that he knew that my wife and I were true and faithful to each other and there was no need to let the strange turn of events ruin my life. I would have to get a new start on living and do the best I could to put the tragedy behind me. I thanked him and went home.

The next day I decided to rent the house furnished, buy a new house and get new furnishings. That helped some because I was not seeing her possessions every day and living in a house that we struggled to get.

HAPPENSTANCE, again.

The company I had once worked for so long asked me what I was doing and if I would be interested in a job with them. I told them I was very happy where I was and making four times the money they had paid me. The manager had some questions about a few new idea projects I was working on when I left the company. They had shelved them and now were interested in pursuing a few of them. He asked if I would have the time to come to the factory for a few days and discuss them. I told him I would be delighted to visit what was left of the factory where I had thoroughly enjoyed working. I also wanted to talk with the employees that were still there. We set a date and I went to the factory. They said to just keep track of my expenses and stay at a good hotel. They would reimburse me plus provide a good amount of day pay. I enjoyed the visit. I almost got back to inventing things.

One of the former employees that lived in an apartment near the factory had lost her husband five years before. I thought I would give her a call and see how she was doing. She asked me what I was doing in the neighborhood and I told her. She said to come over to see her after work so we could talk. She had gotten another assembly job and was making a living.

When I arrived at her apartment she opened the door and I was surprised to see her so scantily clothed. But, I thought, oh well I had known her and her husband for a long time. They had been loyal employees and didn't need much supervision. She made some coffee and set out a bowl of fruit and cookies. We chatted a while and I told her if she ever needed anything to let me know. I told her all about what had happened to me. I said to her, "This is a cozy one room apartment, where do you sleep, on the floor?" She said, "Of course not." She had a murphy bed. She pushed a button and the bed came out of the wall and down to the floor. I remarked that it was quite a contraption and I went over and sort of flung myself back on to it as a spry gesture. She said she could do that too and she sort of jumped on to the bed beside me. I still was not aware of what was about to happen. I told her that when I was in bed with a girl I usually kissed her. She said, "Are you changing your habit?" I said no and kissed her. I said I was out of practice and needed to renew kissing. I felt very peculiar because I had known her husband and he had the utmost respect for me. Here I was in bed with his wife.

We were alone, no one was going to disturb us, so petting seemed the thing to do. I asked her how she felt and she said she didn't mind. It was her first encounter since her husband had passed away. I said, "For me too." We took off all of our clothes and snuggled for a while. You know the old saying about how when one thinks of sex the mind shuts down, so you can understand that it was not too difficult to overcome our embarrassment and enjoy ourselves. It seemed okay to do it, but I had sort of a strange feeling about being there.

She asked me if I wanted to stay all night, but I told her I would like to go back to the hotel. I said I needed to get some sleep and if I stayed with her I suspected neither of us would get any sleep. I told her I would come back the next evening and take her to dinner, which I did. We went back to her place about eight o'clock and tried to push the button again. I was more relaxed this time and she was too, which made it very enjoyable. I had a hard time to get it out of my mind that I was in bed with his wife. I was not used to doing things like that under those conditions.

We spent four nights together and I thoroughly enjoyed her. She was a very nice person, not too well educated, but she knew what life was all about and took things as they came. She was happy to have a job, pay the rent, and just let the world go by. She never got involved in politics or community affairs. She really enjoyed just being herself and not putting on the ritz.

I went back to my job, which was about eighty miles

away and only saw her once in a while. I was working seven days a week running the company. I had seventy-two construction workers and about ten salespeople for whom I was responsible.

One Saturday I called her and asked her to go for dinner, then we would have a few drinks at her place. I would bring a bottle of her favorite wine. She said, "Come on over." When I arrived at her place and she opened the door, she had on a thin blouse and sort of short cut pants, and she was barefoot. Her hair was not combed and I wondered why she looked like that. I sat down at the table and started chatting. She went over and pushed the button and let the bed down. Naturally, I thought she wanted some relaxation before we went to dinner, so I got in to bed with her.

She was very aggressive and I really had a good time satisfying her. She got dressed and we finally went to a family style restaurant and had a good meal. We went back to her place. The bed was still down and I said, come here, let's cuddle. She said, "Aren't you ever satisfied, you came in here and virtually raped me." I was scared. I thought she was drunk, but I knew she had not had a drink since I arrived. I asked her if she was feeling alright and she said yes. I told her I better go because I was not aware of the problem. I asked her if I offended her and she said she didn't like to be pounced on. I never went to see her again because I thought she might be a little loony.

Things were slowing at the company. It was impossible to get a buyer and after trying for six months the owner said to put the business into bankruptcy. We did that and it was auctioned off at about ten cents on the dollar. Which was about what it was worth. The owner kept his funeral home and bought an old motel and converted it in to a home for the elderly. He had made a fortune with the construction company and repair business.

I went to my home town and became a broker/salesman and worked for a broker. I made out quite well and when the opportunity presented itself, I rented a suite in a modern office building and became a Commercial and Industrial Broker. I had met a nice lady in my home town and married her. She was a very intelligent woman and knew how to sell real estate. We listed and sold land for housing developments, sold a golf course and several large parcels of highway land. We bought a house from a builder that was going broke and finished it. We lived in it ten years and sold it at a huge profit.

One day I said to her, "Let's retire and move to Florida." She said she liked it where we lived and was not in favor of moving. She decided to humor me and we spent four months running all over Florida looking for a building lot. We also looked at hundreds of resale and new homes, but none that we really wanted. One day we drove into a housing development of sixty-nine lots with only seven houses on it. I saw the ideal lot in the right town and perfect for the house we wanted to build. My wife designed a three bedroom, two bath, living room, dining room, large kitchen house. The builder was a top notch builder and he did a really good job of building it for us. We added an in-ground lap pool, nine feet wide by thirty feet long, and had a screen enclosure installed around it. You couldn't survive the mosquitoes, snakes and even alligators in season. We did a lavish landscaping job and planted trees, which are now thirty feet tall. We also installed a shallow well lawn sprinkler system. We have a vegetable garden and grow watermelon, cherry tomatoes and a lot of other vegetables. Our source of income is derived from our retirement pensions, Social Security, interest from stocks and bonds, plus we lend money to people building new homes.

Last year we spent over fifty thousand dollars for two new autos. We were driving seventeen-year-old autos because we only drove to town and bowling. We are both in good health and enjoying retirement, thanks to the grace of God and HAPPENSTANCE occurring at the right time. That is why I call this story HAPPENSTANCE.

Epilogue

I trust you enjoyed walking through the time and circumstances that were probably current happenings during the early twentieth century. It is enjoyable to let the mind take you on a pleasant journey through the valley of a wild imagination. It is better than being trapped in a real world of frustration.

Never despair. There are plenty of escape routes.